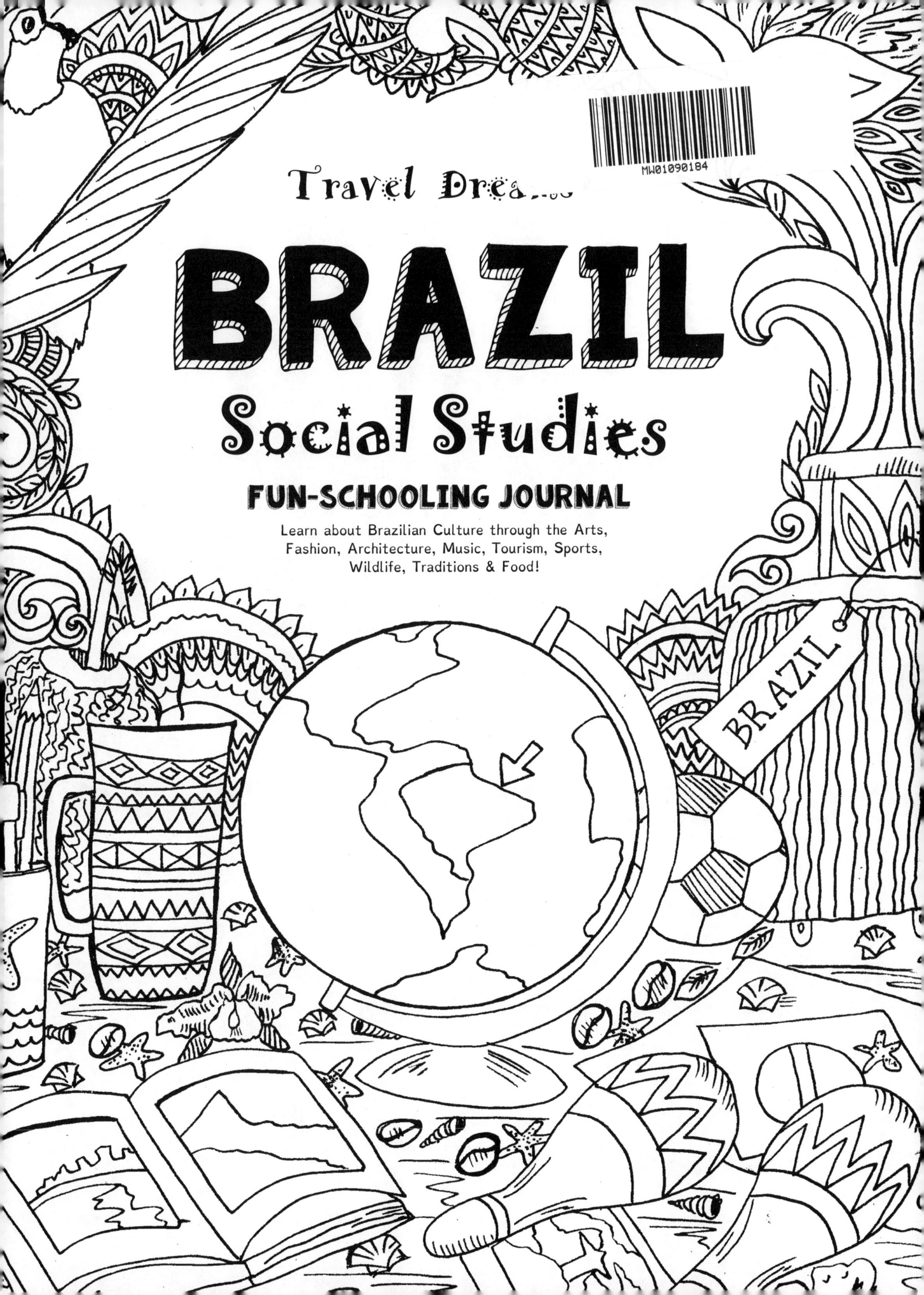
Travel Drea
BRAZIL
Social Studies
FUN-SCHOOLING JOURNAL
Learn about Brazilian Culture through the Arts, Fashion, Architecture, Music, Tourism, Sports, Wildlife, Traditions & Food!
BRAZIL
MW01090184

To hear traditional music from this country listen to

Travel Dreams

Geography

AROUND THE WORLD IN 14 SONGS

Search for Amazon Product Number: B072C2QXJS

Around the world in 14 songs is a delightful musical tour of the world. Adults and children will enjoy these original instrumental songs that reflect the authentic style of music that originated on all six major continents. Travel to the rhythm and melody of traditional instruments, and enjoy the fun-filled tunes.

The musical journey begins in Ireland, sweeps across Europe, dances through Asia, Africa and then soars over the ocean to Australia and the Caribbean! After an exciting night at a Smoky Mountain bluegrass festival you will enjoy a siesta in Mexico and finally land in Brazil where you will join the festa in Rio-De-Janeiro.

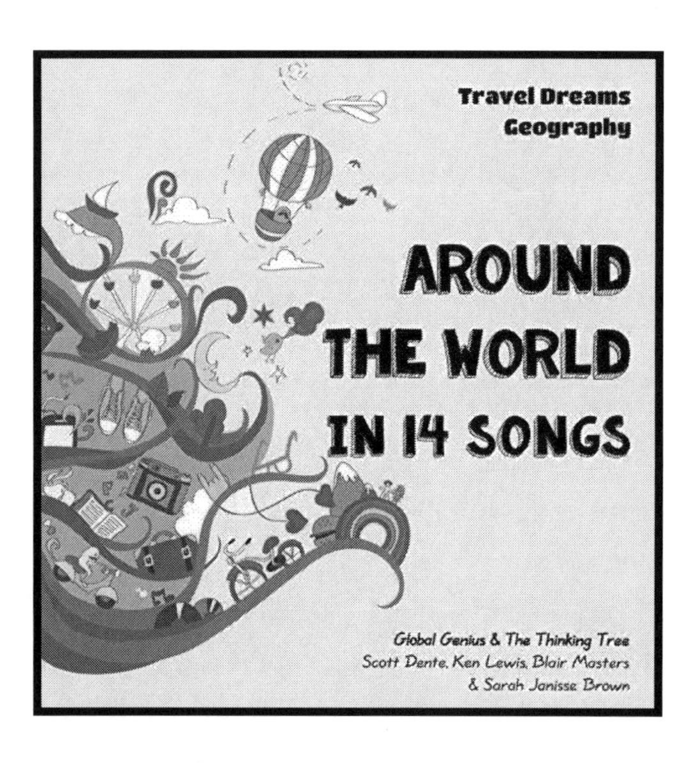

Music has never been more fun... or educational!

Travel Dreams

BRAZIL

FUN-SCHOOLING JOURNAL

An Adventurous Approach

Social Studies

Learn about Brazilian Culture Through the Arts, Fashion, Architecture, Music, Tourism, Sports, Wildlife, Traditions & Food!

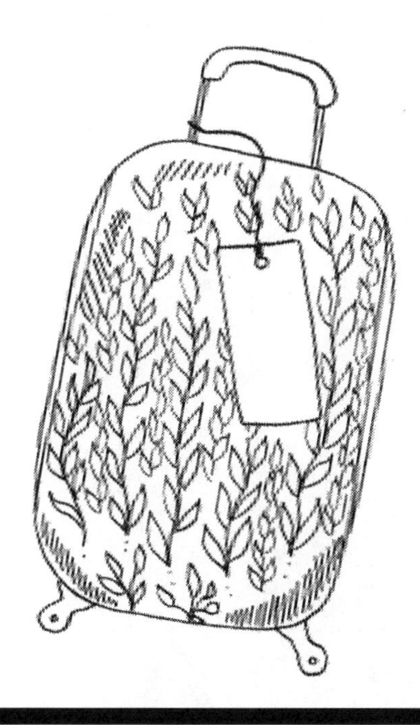

Capoeira
carnival
COFFEE
football
samba
jiu jitsu
Christ
of
Redeemer
orchid
Capoeira
Cachaça
Cachaça
Cachaça
WELCOME TO
Brazil
Brasilia
COFFEE
samba
orchid
Brigadeiro
toco toucan
Rio de Janeiro
Sao Paulo
Caipirinha
Capoeira
carnival
COFFEE
football
samba
jiu jitsu
Christ
of
Redeemer
orchid
Capoeira
Cachaça
Cachaça
Cachaça
WELCOME TO
Brazil
Brasilia
COFFEE
samba
orchid
Brigadeiro
Rio de Janeiro

Travel Dreams BRAZIL Fun-Schooling Journal

Name:

Date:

Contact Information:

About Me:

The Thinking Tree LLC

Let's Learn!

Topics & Activities You Can Explore With This Curriculum:

- Ethnic Cooking
- Travel
- History of Interesting Places
- How People Live
- Tourism
- Transportation
- Wildlife and Natural Wonders
- Cultural Traditions
- Natural Disasters
- Famous and Interesting People
- Missionary Stories
- Scientific Discoveries
- Fashion
- Architecture
- Plants
- Animals
- Maps
- Language

BRAZIL

BRAZIL

5

Travel Dreams Fun-School Journal

You are going to learn about Brazil

Teacher & Parent To-Do List:

- Plan a trip to Brazil or just plan a trip to the library or local bookstore.
- Download Google Earth so your child can zoom in and learn more!
- Choose online videos about Brazil so your child can learn about culture, food, tourism, traditions and history.
- Be prepared to help your child choose an ethnic recipe and shop for the ingredients.

Go to the Library or Bookstore to Pick Out:

- Books about Brazil
- One Atlas or Book of Maps
- One Colorful Cookbook with Recipes from Brazil

DRAW THE COVER OF YOUR BOOKS!

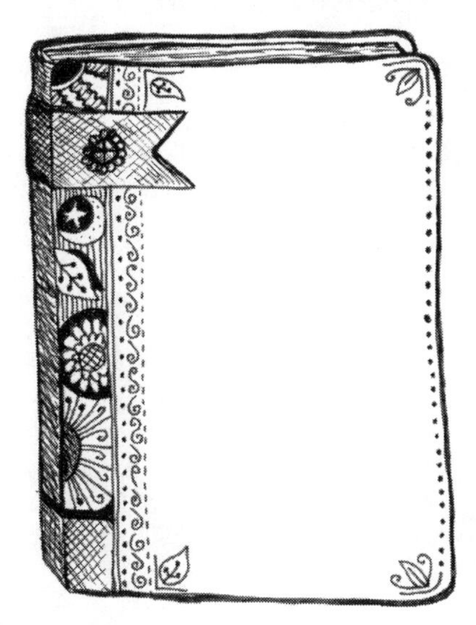

COLOR IN BRAZIL ON THE MAP

Zoom into Brazil using Google Earth and explore the wonders of this amazing country!

LABEL THE MAP

Add 15 Interesting Things to this Map!

Write or Draw

Use your Library Books

Popular Foods:	Traditional Clothing:
Draw the Flag:	A Quote or Proverb:
A Historic Event:	A Famous Landmark:

LEARNING TIME

READ A BOOK AND WATCH A VIDEO ABOUT FOOD IN BRAZIL:

BOOK TITLE:_________________

____

VIDEO TITLE: _________________

____

____

What did you learn?

____

____

____

____

____

____

BRAZILIAN CUISINE

What do Brazilians love to eat?

Can you list 5 of the most popular Brazilian dishes?

1. ______________________________
2. ______________________________
3. ______________________________
4. ______________________________
5. ______________________________
6.

Draw your favorite Brazilian food

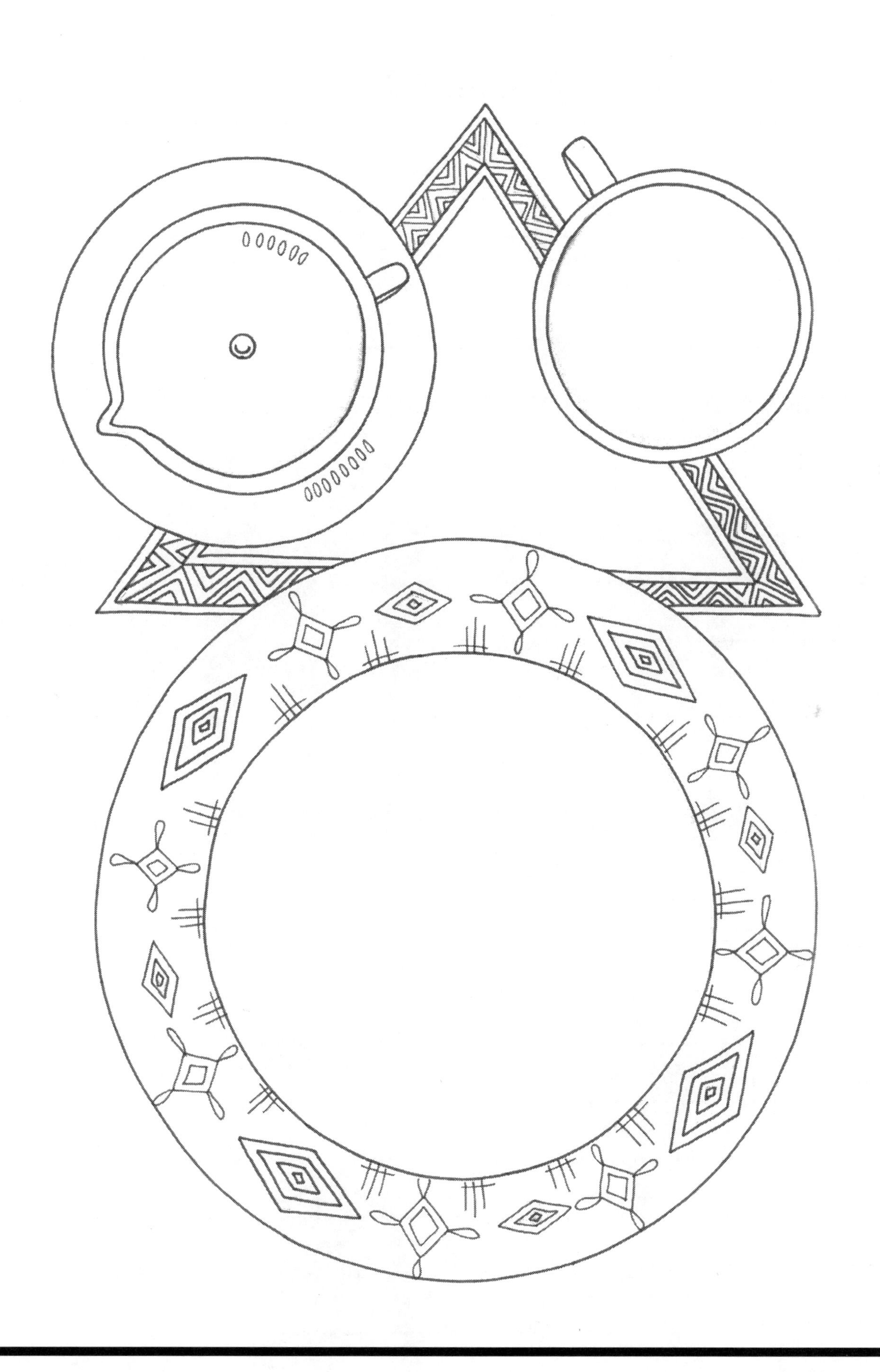

Find a Recipe From

BRAZIL

TITLE:

Ingredients:

Instructions:

Step by Step Food Prep:

1	2
3	4
5	6

DRAW THE FOOD THAT YOU PREPARED!

RATE THE RESULTS! 1, 2, 3, 4, 5

Color the words that best describe your food:

DELICIOUS
YUMMY
TASTY
GREAT
DELIGHTFUL
OKAY
BLAH!
GROSS
YUCKY
DISGUSTING
STINKY
ICKY

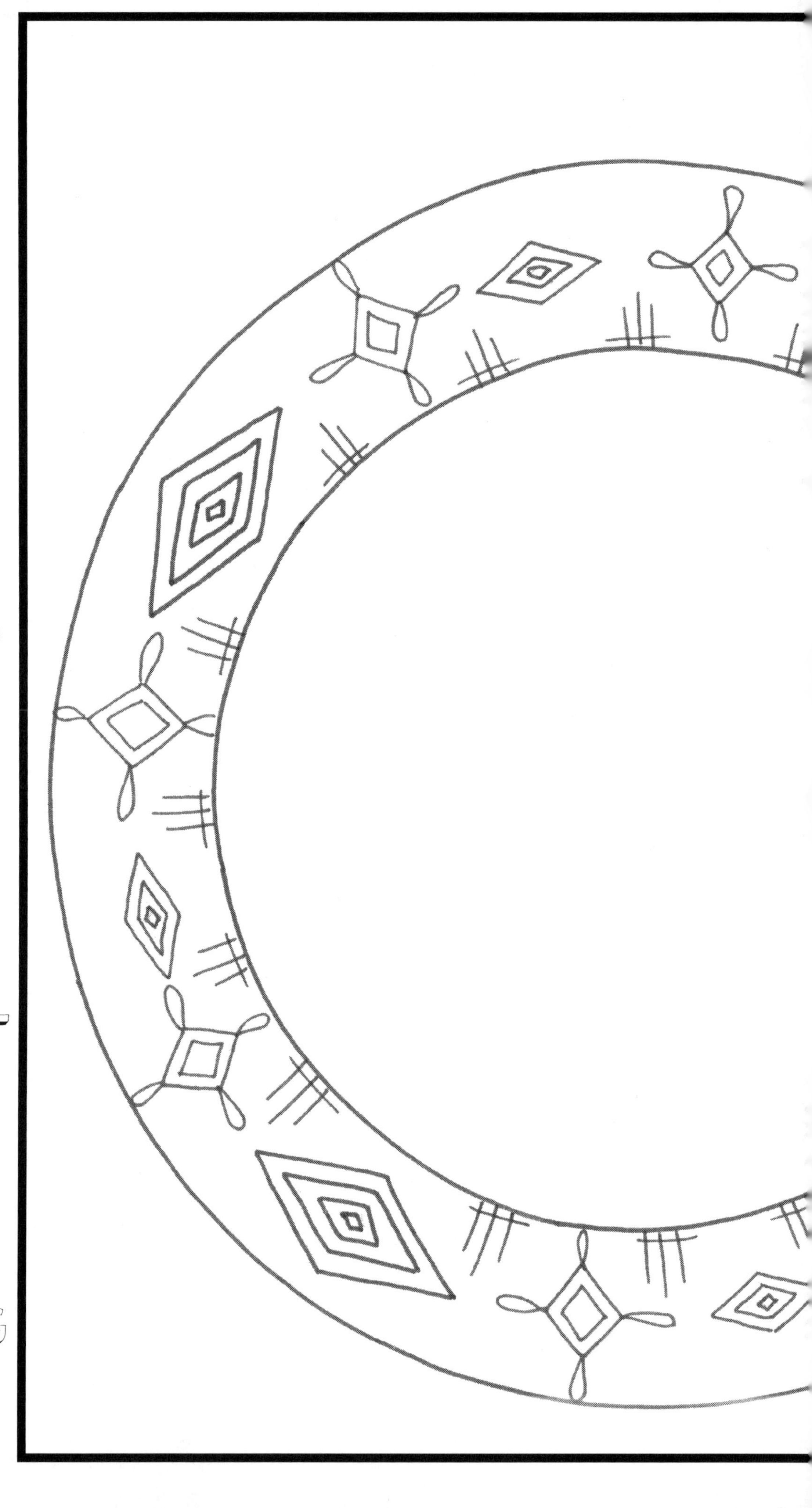

What to Do in Brazil

Create a COMIC STRIP showing your adventure!

LEARNING TIME

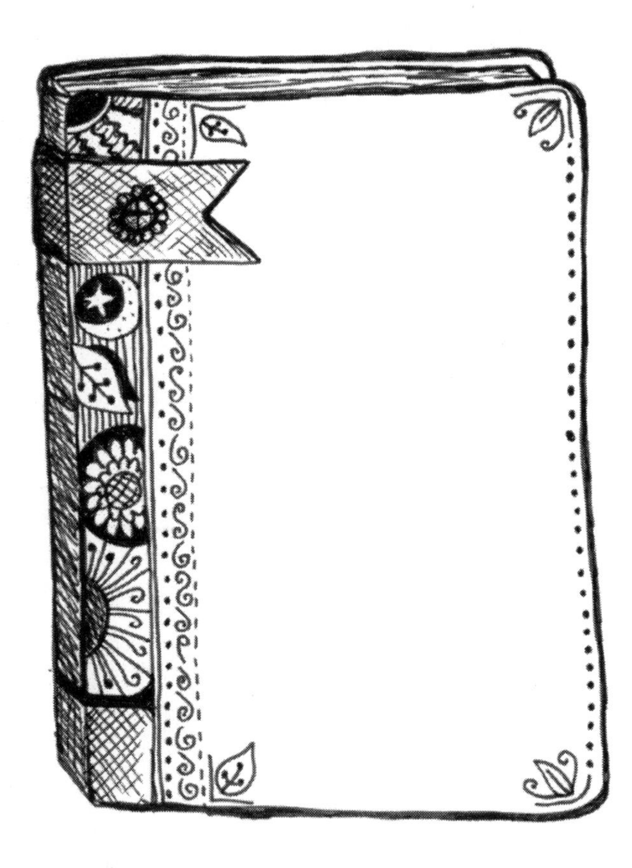

READ A BOOK AND WATCH A VIDEO ABOUT A FAMOUS PERSON

BOOK TITLE: ____________________

____

VIDEO TITLE: ____________________

____

____

Write 3 Interesting Biography Facts

____

____

____

____

____

____

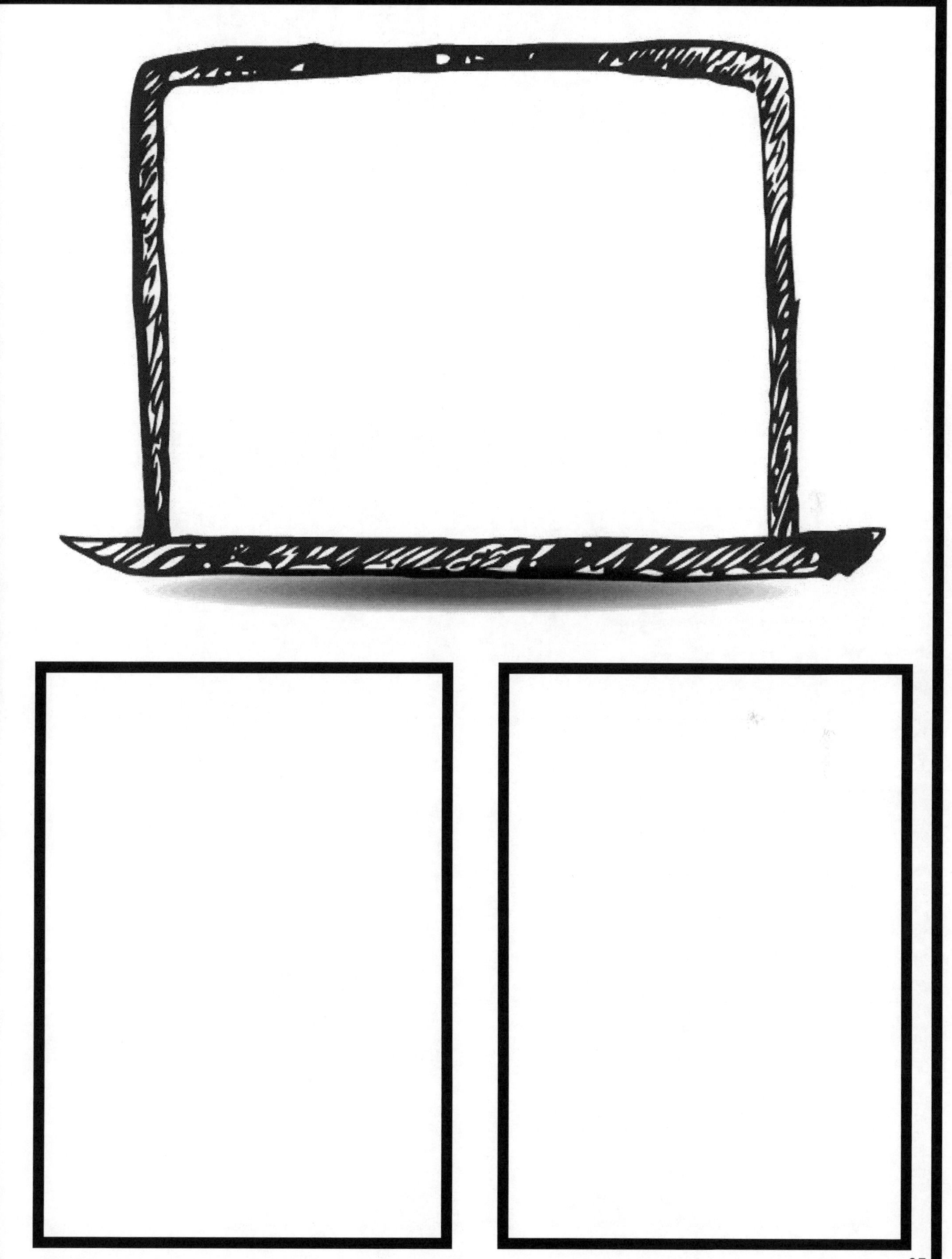

All About Style

BRAZIL

Fashion in the City

MODERN STYLES

Draw yourself dressed like a stylish Brazilian:

Color The Traditional Costume:

Trace and color this traditional Female Brazilian costume

Trace and color this traditional Male Brazilian costume

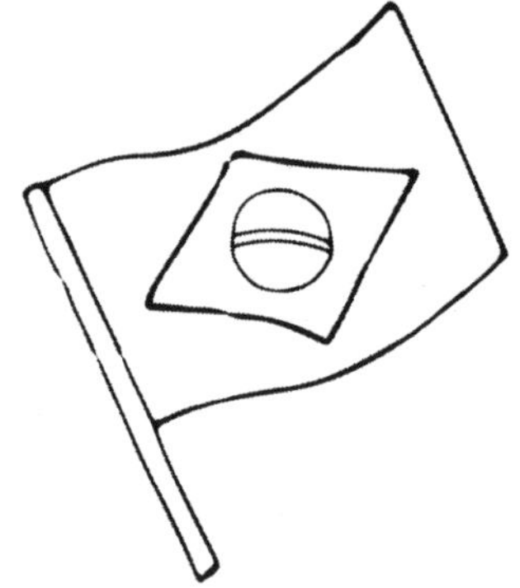

BRAZILIAN HISTORY

Write about a Historic Event

LEARNING TIME

READ A BOOK AND WATCH A VIDEO ABOUT NATURE & WILDLIFE

BOOK TITLE: ____________________

____

VIDEO TITLE: ____________________

____

____

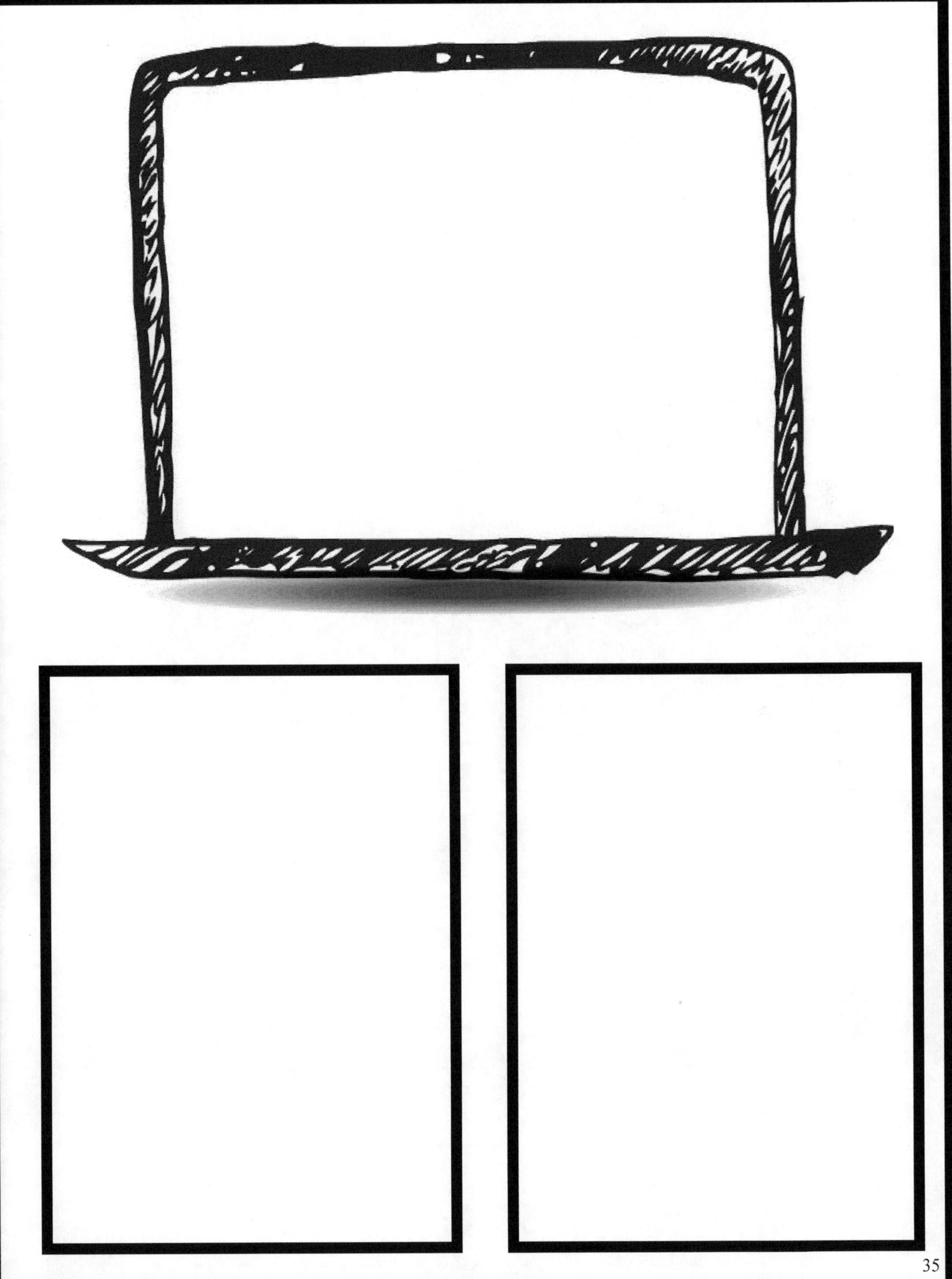

What Animals Live in Brazil?
Can you list ten?

1.____________________________

2.____________________________

3.____________________________

4.____________________________

5.____________________________

6.____________________________

7.____________________________

8.____________________________

9.____________________________

10.___________________________

Draw each of the animals

PLANTS IN BRAZIL

Can you list ten flowers or trees found in Brazil?

1.__________________________
2.__________________________
3.__________________________
4.__________________________
5.__________________________
6.__________________________
7.__________________________
8.__________________________
9.__________________________
10._________________________

Draw each of the plants

HISTORY OF MUSIC IN BRAZIL

Write about a famous Brazilian musician:

What instrument did he/she play?

Can you draw it?

A NATIONAL INSTRUMENT

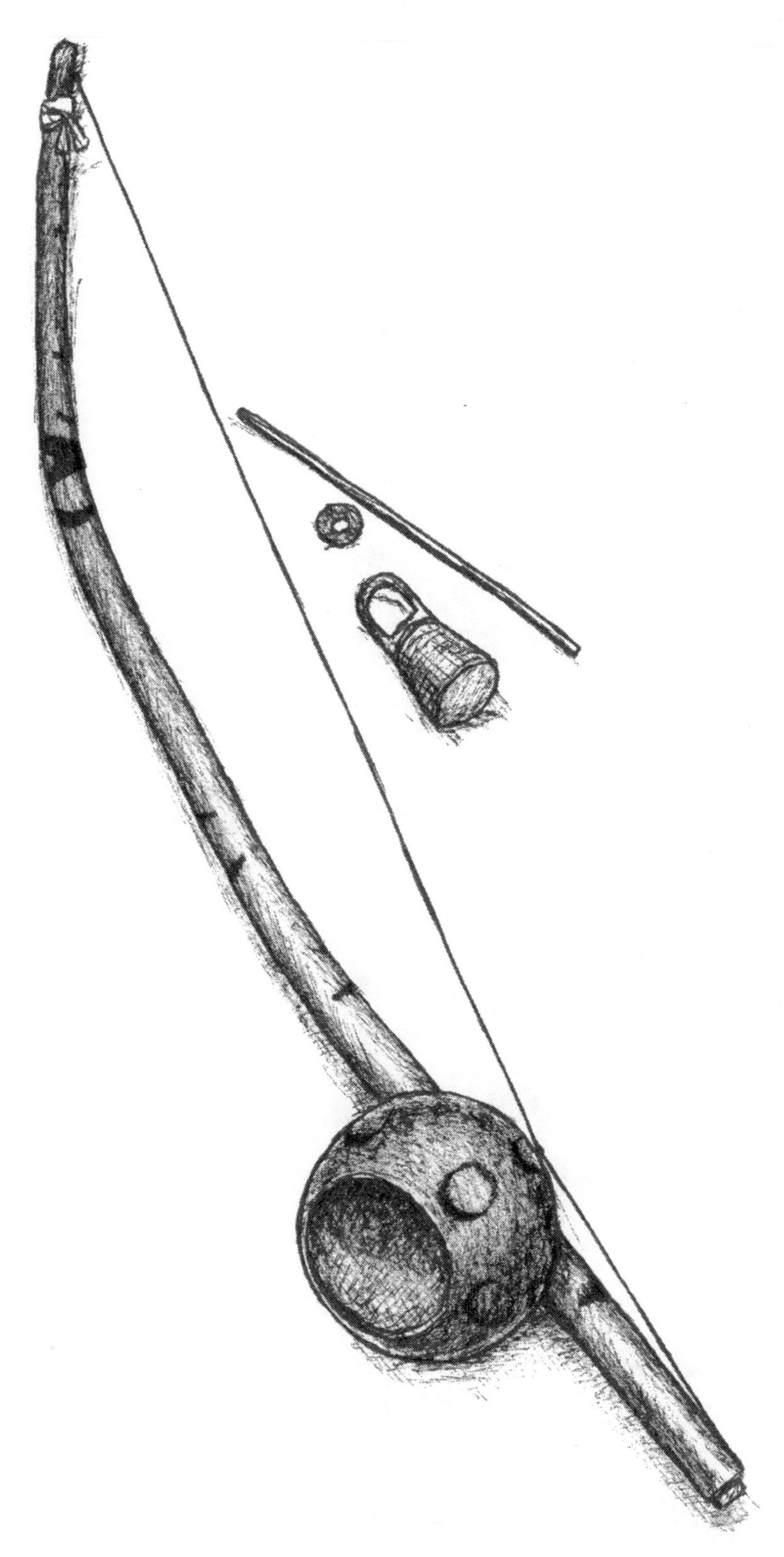

To hear traditional music from this country listen to
Travel Dreams Geography– Around the World in 14 Songs

Track Number & Song Name:
14-Brazil - Festa in Rio-de-Janeiro

BRAZILIAN ART & ENTERTAINMENT

Read a book or Watch a documentary about art and entertainment in Brazil

Write down 5 interesting things you learned :

1. ______________________________

____

2. ______________________________

____

3. ______________________________

____

4. ______________________________

____

5. ______________________________

____

Draw or doodle in Brazilian Style

Write down a quote or
a Lyric From a Famous
Brazilian poem
or Song

HISTORY OF TRANSPORTATION IN BRAZIL

Find 3 interesting Facts about Brazilian transportation

1. ____

____

____

2. ____

____

____

3. ____

____

____

Use your imagination and add something to this picture.

Write a short story about this picture

BRAZILIAN INVENTIONS

Read a book or Watch a documentary about your Favorite Brazilian inventor:

____

Write down 5 interesting things about His/Her Life:

1. ______________________________________

____

2. ______________________________________

____

3. ______________________________________

____

4. ______________________________________

____

5. ______________________________________

____

Write down 3 Brazilian inventions that changed the World:

1. ____________________

2. ____________________

3. ____________________

Draw your Favorite Brazilian invention

BRAZILIAN ATHLETES

Read a book or watch a documentary about your favorite Brazilian athlete:

____

Write down 5 interesting things about his/her life:

1. ______________________________________

2. ______________________________________

3. ______________________________________

4. ______________________________________

5. ______________________________________

Draw a Sport that is popular in Brazil

BRAZILIAN HOMES

Write about a Family tradition in Brazil

BRAZILIAN TRADITIONS

Draw some traditional Brazilian décor elements

Trace & Color

A TRADITIONAL BRAZILIAN HOME

Design Your Own
BRAZILIAN HOME

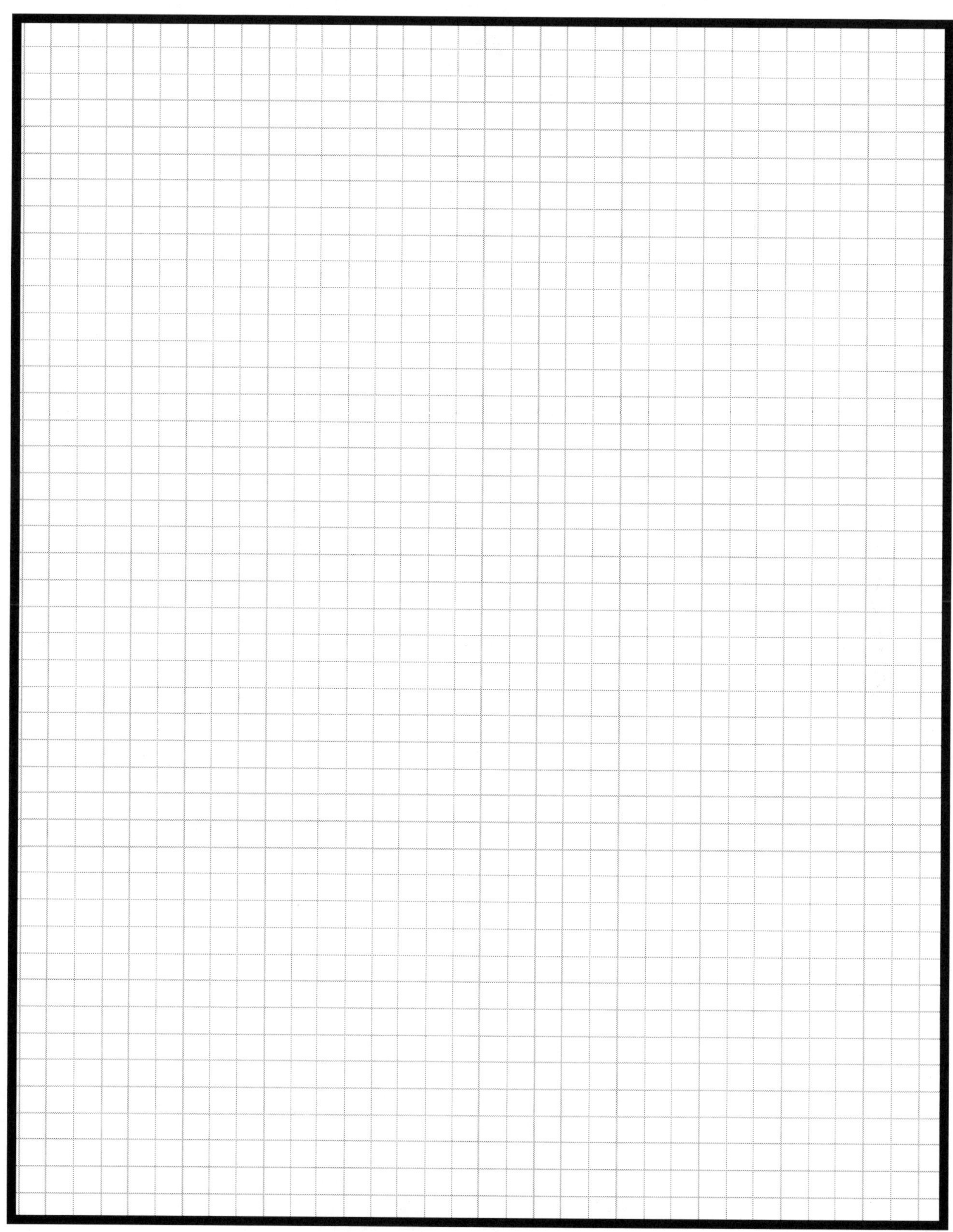

Find and color in the Hidden objects

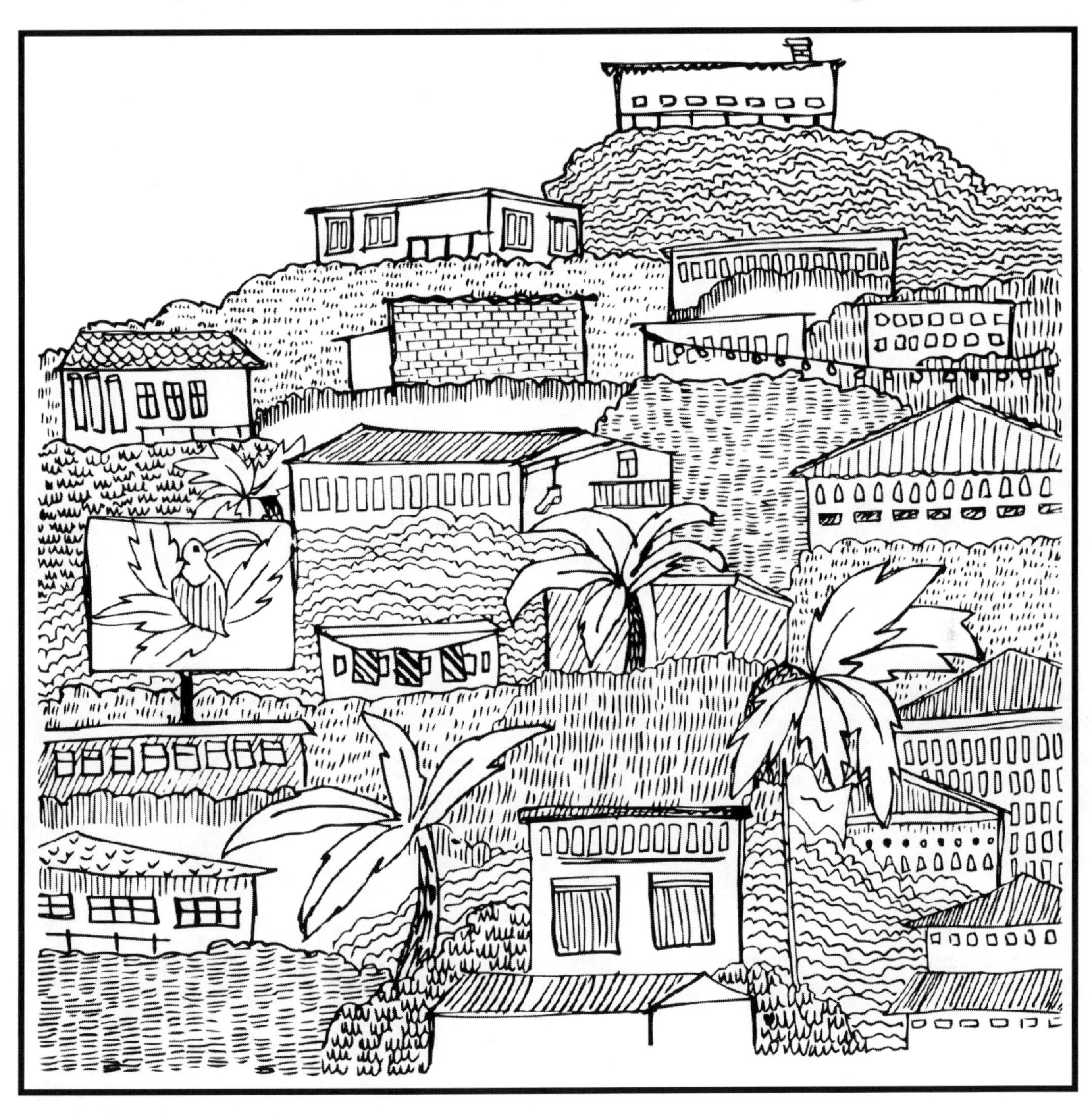

LEARNING TIME

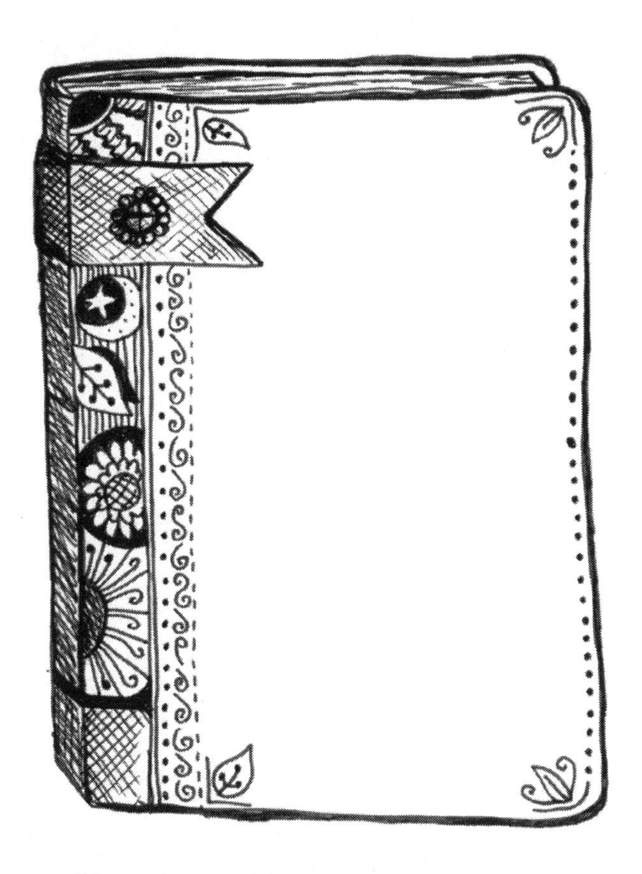

READ A BOOK AND WATCH A VIDEO ABOUT TOURISM & TRAVEL

BOOK TITLE: ____________________

____

VIDEO TITLE: ____________________

____

____

PLAN A TRIP TO THE CAPITAL OF BRAZIL

_ _ _   _ _   _ _ _ _ _ _ _

Who are you going with?

What are you taking with you?

How long is your trip?

What do you want to see or visit?

PLAN YOUR TRIP

What to Do in Rio De Janeiro

Five Things to Know when Traveling to BRAZIL

1 ______________________________

2 ______________________________

3 ______________________________

4 ______________________________

5 ______________________________

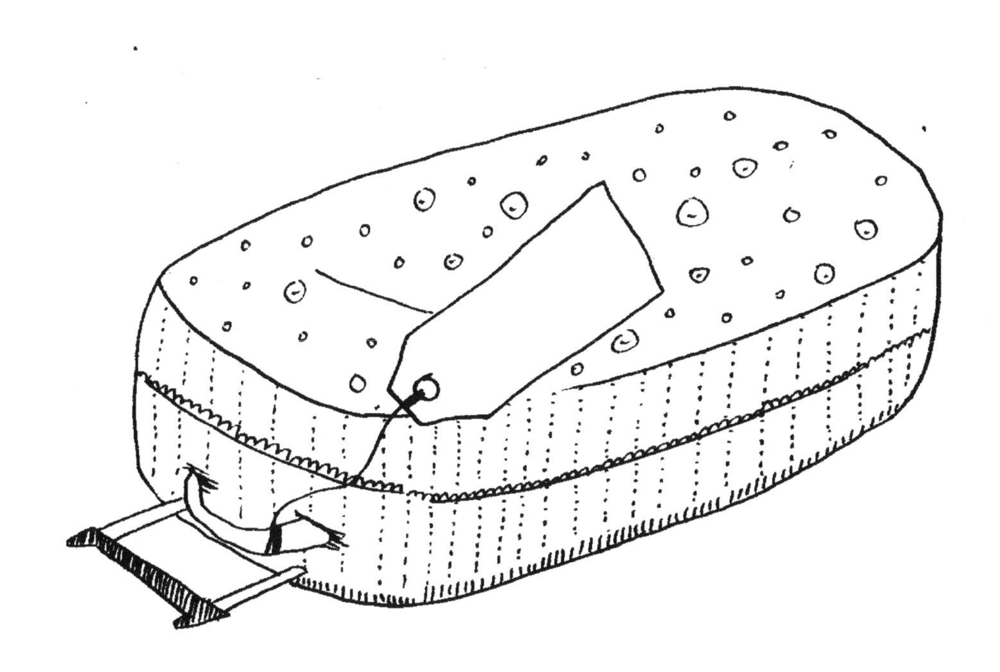

What to Say

Create a **COMIC STRIP** using six Brazilian phrases:

CREATIVE WRITING

Write a story about an imaginary trip to Brazil

Illustrate your Story

Do it Yourself HOMESCHOOL JOURNALS

BY THE THINKING TREE, LLC

FunSchoolingBooks.com

DyslexiaGames.com

Contact Us: jbrown@DyslexiaGames.com

THE Thinking TREE
PUBLISHING COMPANY
Sarah Janisse Brown
ART
LOGIC
SCIENCE
SPELLING
READING
COLORING
THINKING
DRAWING
CREATING

Made in United States
Orlando, FL
10 January 2025